ALICE OSE

HEARTSTOPPER

VOLUME 1

D0462336

HODDER CHILDREN'S BOOKS

First published by the author as a Kickstarter edition in 2018
This edition published in 2019 by Hodder and Stoughton

37

Text and illustrations copyright © Alice Oseman, 2018

The moral rights of the author have been asserted.

All characters and events in this publication, other than those clearly
in the public domain, are fictitious and any resemblance to
real persons, living or dead, is purely coincidental.

All rights reserved.
No part of this publication may be reproduced, stored in
a retrieval system, or transmitted, in any form or by any means, without
the prior permission in writing of the publisher, nor be otherwise circulated
in any form of binding or cover other than that in which it is published
and without a similar condition including this condition being
imposed on the subsequent purchaser.

Please be aware that this book contains depictions of physical assault and verbal homophobia.

This comic is drawn digitally using a Wacom Intuos Pro small tablet directly into Photoshop CC.

A CIP catalogue record for this book
is available from the British Library.

ISBN 978 1 444 95138 7

Printed and bound in Great Britain by
Clays Ltd, Elcograf S.p.A.

The paper and board used in this book
are made from wood from responsible sources.

Hodder Children's Books
An imprint of
Hachette Children's Group
Part of Hodder and Stoughton
Carmelite House
50 Victoria Embankment
London EC4Y 0DZ

An Hachette UK Company
www.hachette.co.uk

www.hachettechildrens.co.uk

www.aliceoseman.com

CONTENTS

1. MEET

January

TICK

TICK

TICK

TICK

TICK

TICK

TICK

TICK

2

3

YAWN

8

A COMIC BY

ALICE
OSEMAN

DAY 2

All right?

...All right.

DAY 3

morning ^‿^

morning

DAY 4

Hey!

Hey

19

23

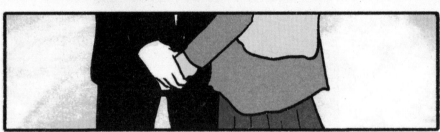

February

33

Hey, Charlie

I need to talk to you.

Erm... I have a drum lesson right now

Answer my fucking texts, then! It's been two weeks!

I already said I don't want to meet up with you anymore.

40

41

beep

beep
beep
The bell? Lunch is over already?
FUCK I'm missing my drum lesson!
Can I think about it?
Yeah, sure!

Charlie Spring, though?

45

46

49

MISS SINGH. P.E. TEACHER. EX SEMI-PRO RUGBY PLAYER.

So. You're the chosen one.

um

52

53

...So we've covered passing and scoring...

We've got about 15 minutes left, so-

-do you want to give tackling a go?

...Tackling?

55

I am definitely **way** too weak to do that

Excuse me – where is your 'can do' attitude?

Give it a go. Just run at me. I won't dodge!

Go onnnn. I bet you can do it.

...Fine

TWO DAYS LATER...

FIVE DAYS LATER...

61

He's been doing really well, hasn't he!

You're surprised?

Well all I knew about him was that he's gay

Mate, I don't actually think being gay makes you bad at sports.

I never said that!! Anyway, I can see why he's popular. He's managed to fit in really well.

Yeah... he's just a really cool guy! :)

62

64

65

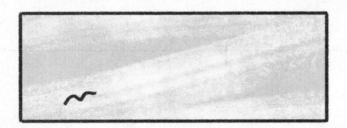

PHYSICAL EDUCATION

ignore me!!!!!

Today

You're at rugby, right? Meet me in the music block afterwards

Why?

Please Charlie I want to talk

Why would <u>I</u> be scared? Everyone in the school already knows I'm gay! YOU'RE the one who's scared of getting caught! You're not even my boyfriend! I've seen you with your girlfriend at the school gate!!

You don't give a SHIT about me. You just found the nearest guy who was willing to make out with you and went for it!

<u>YOU</u> went for it too. Don't be angry at me for not wanting to come out yet.

I'm not angry about that! I'm angry because you never even slightly cared about my feelings at <u>all</u>. We only ever meet up when you want, where you want—

When you feel like making out with a boy!

I could be ANYONE! You don't give a shit!

That's obviously not true

It is <u>true</u>! You just heard the rumours about me and were like "Oh good, there's finally a gay boy I can safely get off with"!!

SLAM

84

Are you okay?

I just... kind of followed you... You seemed really stressed out while we were getting changed.

I just started getting worried... er... so... yeah.

FIVE MINUTES EARLIER

Get off—

Stop it

PAT

PAT
PAT

?

Come on, we'll get locked in if we stay here much longer

PAT

2. CRUSH

tap
tap tap

"Hey, did you hear some Year 9 has come out as gay?"

TEN MONTHS AGO...

99

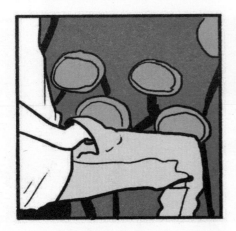

Nick Nelson
Hey, just wanted to check you're okay. Ben's such a dick!!!

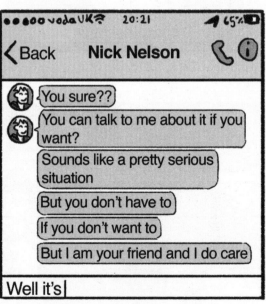

But you don't have to
If you don't want to
But I am your friend and I do care

 Charlie Spring
Okay
Might be a bit of a long story lol

Nick Nelson
I don't mind!!

 Well it started last September

Everyone at school had found out I was gay by then. the bullying had mostly stopped I guess and people had started to be nice to me (there was a group of Sixth Formers who stopped the bullies) but everyone in the school knew i was gay.

So I was practising my drums one morning before form in a practice room and I look up and see Ben looking in through the door window. He walks in and starts telling me how good I am at playing the drums, and I'm just sitting there like 'what the fuck' because I've never spoken to him before in my life… but also kind of freaking out because I thought he was really attractive…

Eventually he comes in and sits next to me and starts talking to me about me coming out at school, and like, how 'brave' I am and stuff… even though it's not like I came out myself or anything, it just got out because I told a couple of people…

And then next thing I know he's just kissing me

And yeah, we just continued to meet up sometimes at school before form. And like… I was so excited about it. I thought I had a boyfriend, or, like, I was having some big romance… But I slowly started to realise he was just using me for someone to make out with… because I was the only gay boy he knew…

and then in January I found out he had a girlfriend as well. Some girl from Higgs school. I don't know if he's bisexual or gay or whatever but it doesn't really change anything. He was just using me.

tap
tap tap

I tried to end it but he just kept pestering me. I thought I'd just meet up with him one last time to tell him to leave me alone but… yeah. That didn't go well I guess haha

111

tap

tap

tap

Nick Nelson
FUCK I hate Ben so much. I knew he was a dick, but... jesus.

Please don't ever talk to him again

Charlie Spring
I definitely won't!!!!

Nick Nelson
I will kick his ass if he tries to come near you

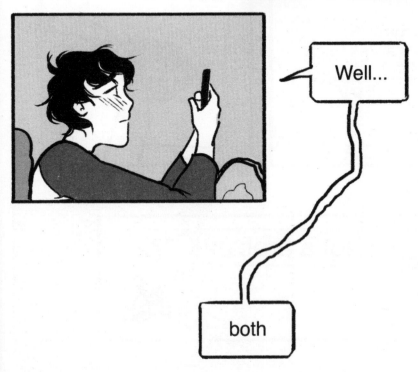

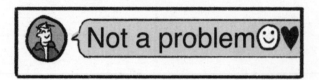

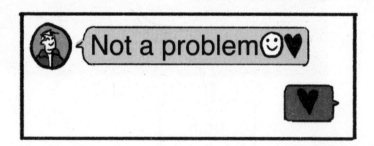

Should I
have told him
all that?

SATURDAY

131

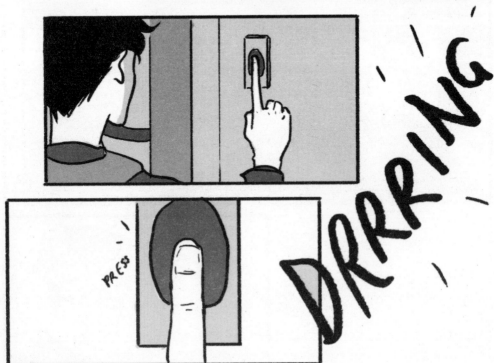

135

It's snowing

Sorry I don't have any joggers to give you, I think they'd all be too big haha...

You should probably go and sit on a radiator for a bit!

CLICK

FSSShh

?

Charlie seems like a lovely boy. When did you meet him?

A couple of months ago. He's in my form group.

157

Are you okay?

I fell for a straight boy... haha...

THE NEXT SATURDAY

KNOCK

KNOCK

165

There, you're a pro now!

...

...

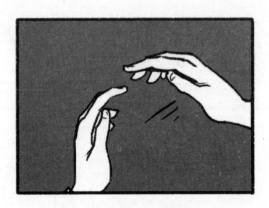

ROLL

175

176

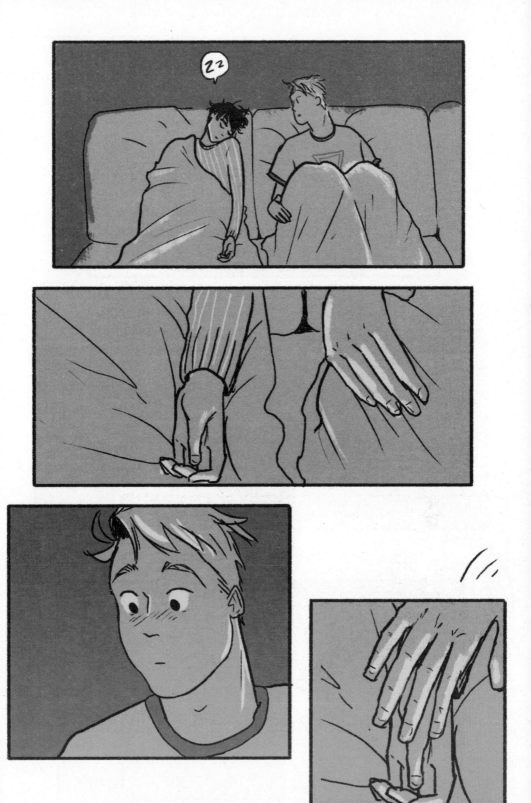

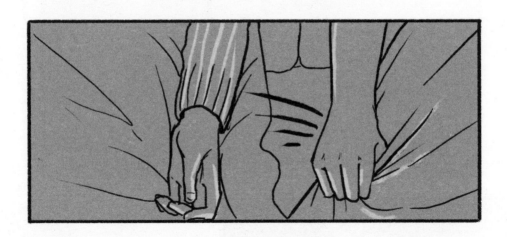

BLINK
BLINK

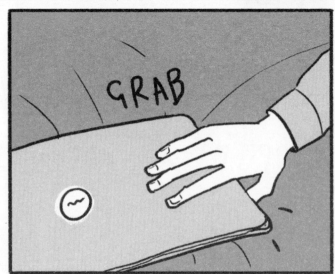

GRAB

CLENCH

TAP
TAP

TAP

Searc
UK

am i gay?

tap tap tap

search

UK

i like girls but now i like a boy????

HOVER

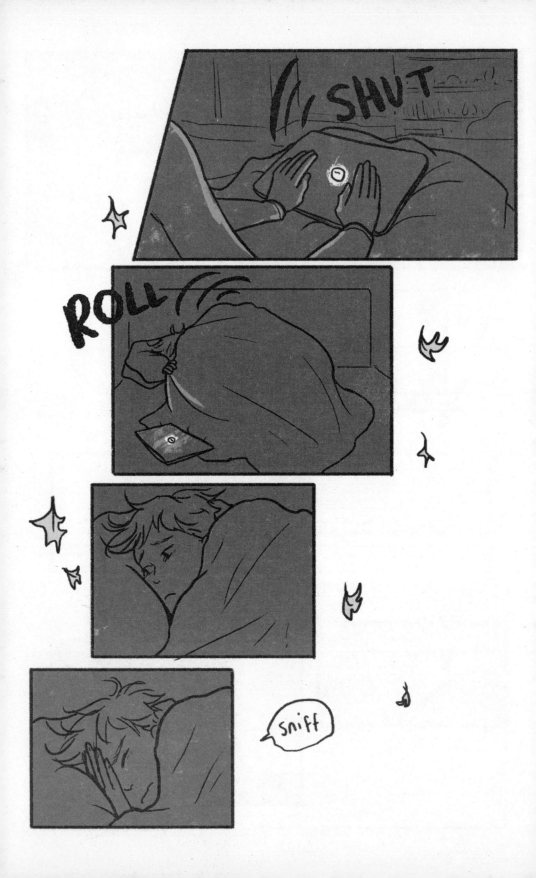

help me...

APRIL
(TWO WEEKS LATER)

Hey Tao... so... about Nick Nelson

What??? Has something happened???

Well... I think he might maybe like me back

EXPLAIN.

Over the past two weeks during the Easter holidays we've hung out like almost EVERY DAY

He's a lot more... idk... physical? We hug now?

Sometimes I just catch him looking at me...

200

... Charlie... I didn't
. I've asked around
a crush on a girl ca
ggs school for, like,

30 MINS LATER...

CHRISTIAN   SAI   OTIS

But Nick's not gay, is he?

Well, I guess we don't know

He doesn't <u>look</u> gay. And didn't he have a crush on that girl Tara Jones?

MISS SINGH (P.E. TEACHER AND COACH)

You can't tell whether people are gay by what they look like.

And gay or straight aren't the only two options.

Anyway, it's very rude to speculate about people's sexuality.

Go home, lads.

I can kinda see it. Nick and Charlie.

Are you going to Harry Greene's party on Saturday?

206

It's so loud in here! D'you wanna go get a drink?

Yeah Sure!

BAR→

NO ALCOHOL

Hey Nick!!

214

215

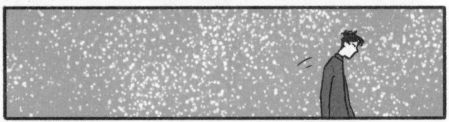

221

er... well...

You can always talk to me about it if you need to...

...

Where did he go?

um...
Sorry...

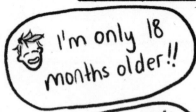

exhale

So...like...

Was Harry being serious? Do you like that girl?

239

NO! No, definitely not!

We... we kissed at a party when we were like 13 and I liked her at the time but I've honestly barely thought about her since then and I DEFINITELY don't like her that way anymore!

Ah... Okay...

241

...I've asked around...
had a crush on a girl cal...
Higgs school for like, 3 ye...

Haha... what's she like, then?

...

You're just gonna assume they're a she?

249

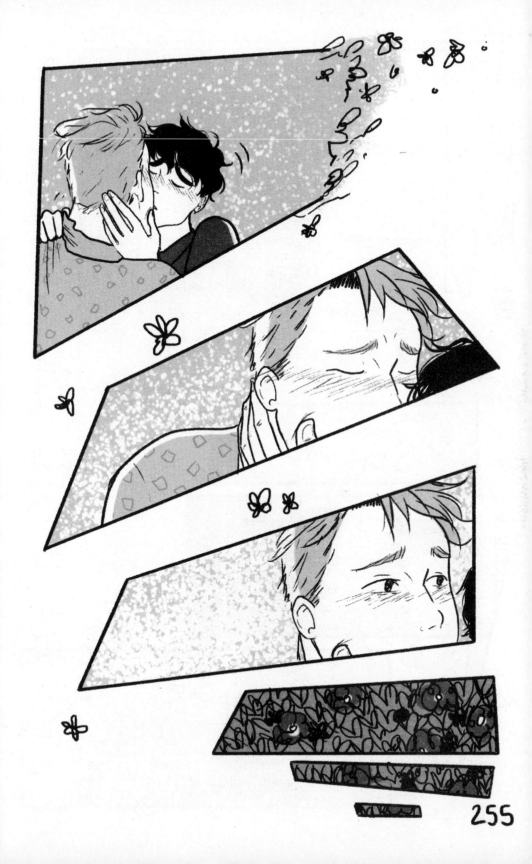

you okay?

I-

Nick? Are you up here?

SHUT

I'm sorry

I'm sorry

I'm sorry

Heartstopper will continue in Volume 2!

Read more of the comic online:

heartstoppercomic.tumblr.com
tapas.io/series/heartstopper

SCHOOL UNIFORM:

1. TIES
Truham students in Years 7-11 wear a plain navy tie. When they get into sixth form (Years 12-13), they get to wear a stripy tie!

2. SCHOOL CREST
The school crest is a fairly simple design! T for Truham and two spades symbols.

3. JUMPER
Truham students have the option of a grey jumper or cardigan. Nick prefers to just wear a shirt, while Charlie likes to wear a jumper or cardigan because he's always cold!

4. BLAZER
Truham students have to wear a blazer unless they're in a lesson. Rolling up the sleeves isn't allowed but lots of students do it anyway!

5. SHOES
Any shoes are allowed, as long as they're smart and black. That means no trainers!

RUGBY UNIFORM:

1. COLOURS
Their rugby uniform mainly consists of a striped navy/light blue rugby shirt. They only wear their uniform for official matches, though.

2. SHORTS
The team usually just wear their P.E. shorts for matches. Charlie doesn't enjoy this during the winter.

3. SOCKS
Players are supposed to wear long navy sports socks for matches. As you can see, Charlie is yet to get himself a pair.

4. SHOES
Nick loves rugby, so he has his own pair of studded rugby boots. Charlie isn't so passionate about the sport so he just sticks with a pair of Vans.

A

Boyfriend - Best Coast
Everywhere - Fleetwood Mac
In2 - WSTRN
What's It Gonna Be? - Shura
Style - Taylor Swift
What Would You Say - The Tin Pigeons
Hot - Avril Lavigne
Young Adult Friction - The Pains of Being Pure at Heart
I Want To Hold Your Hand - The Beatles
Sleepover - Hayley Kiyoko

B

LOVE. FEAT. ZACARI - Kendrick Lamar
Summertime Clothes - Animal Collective
I Wanna Be Your Boyfriend - Discovery
Let Me - ZAYN
8TEEN - Khalid
It's Alright 2 Cry - Francis and the Lights
WILD - Troye Sivan
PILLOWTALK - ZAYN
Into You - Ariana Grande
Anyone Else But You - The Moldy Peaches

Saturday 20th March

Hung out with Charlie all day!! He came over and we went out in the snow with Nellie which was so much fun!! I really like hanging out with Charlie, like WAY more than my other friends. I feel like I can actually just relax and be myself around him, and we still have such a good time and joke around, I swear I can't stop smiling when we're hanging out. I know it's weird but I honestly don't think I've ever liked a friend this much before... I sort of dread seeing my other friends, like they're kind of annoying and being around them is stressful.

But when I'm with Charlie I don't want the day to end??

20/3

So today was amazing - Nick invited me round his house to meet his dog Nellie and I ended up hanging out there all afternoon! It started snowing so we went out into the field behind his house with Nellie and we just mucked about in the snow for ages. It was so much fun but GOD my heart can't deal with being around him for that long... there was this one moment when we came inside and I was really wet and cold so he wrapped me in a blanket and I swear I nearly melted on the spot...

~~Little Maybe~~ UGH sometimes I get the impression he might like me back but... idk maybe he's just really friendly.

ARRRGH why did I have to fall for a straight boy :(

NAME:
CHARLES SPRING

NICKNAME:
CHARLIE

WHO ARE YOU:
NICK'S FRIEND

SCHOOL YEAR:
YEAR 10

AGE:
14

BIRTHDAY:
APRIL 27TH

MBTI:
ISTP

FUN FACT:

I LOVE TO
READ!

NAME:
Nicholas Nelson

NICKNAME:
Nick

WHO ARE YOU:
Charlie's friend

SCHOOL YEAR:
Year 11

AGE:
16

BIRTHDAY:
September 4th

MBTI:
ESFJ

FUN FACT:

I'm great at
baking cakes

NAME:
Tao Xu

NICKNAME:
Tao
WHO ARE YOU:
Charlie's friend
SCHOOL YEAR:
Year 10
AGE:
15
BIRTHDAY:
September 23rd
MBTI:
ENFP
FUN FACT:
I have a film review blog

NAME:
VICTORIA SPRING

NICKNAME:
TORI
WHO ARE YOU:
CHARLIE's SISTER
SCHOOL YEAR:
YEAR 11
AGE:
16
BIRTHDAY:
APRIL 5TH
MBTI:
INFJ
FUN FACT:

I HATE (ALMOST)

EVERYONE

NAME:
Benjamin Hope

NICKNAME:
Ben
WHO ARE YOU:
Charlie's ex
SCHOOL YEAR:
Year 11
AGE:
16
BIRTHDAY:
December 1st
MBTI:
ENTP
FUN FACT:

I can skateboard

NAME:
Tara Jones

NICKNAME:
Tara
WHO ARE YOU:
Nick's old crush
SCHOOL YEAR:
Year 11
AGE:
15
BIRTHDAY:
July 3rd
MBTI:
INFP
FUN FACT:

I love dance!
(especially ballet)

NAME:
HARRY GREENE

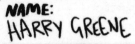

NICKNAME:
HARRY
WHO ARE YOU:
NICK'S CLASSMATE
SCHOOL YEAR:
YEAR 11
AGE:
16
BIRTHDAY:
APRIL 17TH
MBTI:
ESTJ
FUN FACT:

I HAVE OVER 20k
INSTA FOLLOWERS

NAME:
Nellie Nelson

NICKNAME:
Nellie
WHO ARE YOU:
Nick's dog
SCHOOL YEAR:
N/A
AGE:
65 (dog years)
BIRTHDAY:
Unknown
MBTI:
ESFP
FUN FACT:

Boof!

Author's note

Nick and Charlie have been in my heart for a very long time.

As many of you know, they both first appeared in my debut YA novel, 'Solitaire'.
Charlie is the younger brother of the narrator, Tori, and Nick is his doting,
protective boyfriend. Neither of them are particularly major characters, but in the
novel, aged 17 and 15 respectively, they are in a firm, loving, supportive relationship.
That's where my desire to tell their story began. How did they get to this point?
And where will they go from here?

In my spare time during my A-Levels, I filled an entire sketchbook with my first
attempt at telling the backstory of Nick and Charlie. Then I started again, my art
slightly better, and filled another sketchbook with a second attempt at
the comic. I remember spending hours at a time just sitting and drawing in
bed, not even listening to music in the background, completely lost and in love
with the story of Nick and Charlie. It brought me peace in a
way not even writing my novels could.

In 2016, aged twenty-one and my art greatly improved, I launched Heartstopper.
It started small, but slowly its audience grew and grew. At the time of editing this
author's note, Heartstopper has over 70,000 followers across Tumblr and Tapas.
People come to the story for all sorts of reasons - for the realistic romance, for the
LGBT+ rep, for the art, for the drama. But I think most of all people have
been drawn to Heartstopper because it brings them comfort.

It brings me that too.

Alice x

From a Nick and Charlie comic I drew in 2013

Love and thanks to my Patreon patrons, Kickstarter supporters,
and all readers of HEARTSTOPPER over the past couple of years.
This book wouldn't have been possible without you.

A huge thanks also to my agent, Claire Wilson, to my editor, Rachel Wade,
and to the whole team at Hachette Children's. Thank you for showing
HEARTSTOPPER so much love.

Finally, a special shout-out to those amazing people who gave a
little more to the Kickstarter:

JT Taylor, Lorna Burch, Kyle Sanders, Ade Mayr,
Ruben Molina Fernandez, Lucy Powrie, Shannon Baillie, Annie Furlong-Muir,
David Browne, Isobel, Lucy McGlasson, Jake Fraser, Charlotte Dreyfus,
Manon Pothin, Lowen Crombie, Chloe Zargarpour, Liang Hai, Katie Gibson,
Whitney Gravelle, Daphne Tonge (Illumicrate), Tory Schorsch, Jamie Destouet,
Janintserani Herrera, Peter Stromberg, Elise Buchanan,
Bella Beecham, Orlee Pnini, and John H. Bookwalter Jr.

ALSO BY ALICE OSEMAN:

SOLITAIRE

Read the novel Nick and Charlie first appeared in!

A pessimistic sixteen-year-old girl, a teenage speed skater with a penchant for solving mysteries, and a series of anonymous pranks at school by an online group who call themselves 'Solitaire'.

Alice's debut novel tells the story of Tori Spring.

RADIO SILENCE

Everyone thinks seventeen-year-old Frances is destined for a top university - including herself. But, in secret, Frances spends all her free time drawing fan art for a sci-fi podcast, 'Universe City'. And when she discovers that the creator of the podcast lives opposite her, Frances begins to question everything she knew about herself and what she wants from life.

What if everything you set yourself up to be was wrong?

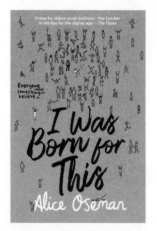

I WAS BORN FOR THIS

Angel, a massive fangirl of boyband The Ark, is headed to London to see The Ark live for the first time. Jimmy, frontman of The Ark, is struggling to deal with how famous he and his bandmates are becoming.

Over one week in August, Angel and Jimmy's lives begin to intertwine in mysterious ways, and when Angel and Jimmy are unexpectedly thrust together, they will discover just how strange and surprising facing up to reality can be.